TEN HUNGRY TURKEYS

TILDA BALSLEY   ILLUSTRATED BY ILENE RICHARD

PELICAN PUBLISHING COMPANY

GRETNA 2018

The word "Pelican" and the depiction of a pelican are trademarks of Pelican Publishing Company, Inc., and are registered in the U.S. Patent and Trademark Office.

Library of Congress Cataloging-in-Publication Data

Names: Balsley, Tilda, author. | Richard, Ilene, illustrator.
Title: Ten hungry turkeys / by Tilda Balsley ; illustrated by Ilene Richard.
Description: Gretna : Pelican Publishing Company, 2017. | Summary: "Mr. and
   Mrs. Chris P. Byrd are planning a big lunch on Thursday, and they invite
   ten turkeys to come early. However, one by one the turkeys drop out, as
   they wonder what this is really about"— Provided by publisher.
Identifiers: LCCN 2016003403| ISBN 9781455622351 (hardcover : alk. paper) |
   ISBN 9781455622368 (e-book)
Subjects: | CYAC: Stories in rhyme. | Counting—Fiction. | Turkeys—Fiction.
   | Thanksgiving—Fiction.
Classification: LCC PZ8.3.B2185 Te 2017 | DDC [E]—dc23 LC record available at
https://lccn.loc.gov/2016003403

Printed in Malaysia
Published by Pelican Publishing Company, Inc.
1000 Burmaster Street, Gretna, Louisiana 70053
www.pelicanpub.com

To Jacob, Boyd, Sloan, and Jane—remembering happy Thanksgivings!

Dear Turkeys,

We're planning a big lunch on Thursday.

Please come early. It wouldn't be any fun without you.

Love,

Mr. and Mrs. Chris P. Byrd

Ten feathered friends said, "Oh boy, an invitation!"
Ten feathered friends said, "Sounds like a celebration!"
They flapped their wings around the yard,
and stamped their bony feet.

One wrote back "Great!
We won't be late,
and thank you for this treat."

TEN hungry turkeys were on their way to lunch
when one turkey said, "Uh oh, I have a hunch.
I know we thought this would be fun,
but something just feels wrong.

Please don't be mad,
'cause I feel bad.
I just can't come along."

NINE hungry turkeys were on their way to lunch
when one turkey said, "Uh oh, I have a hunch.
The falling leaves and chilly air
mean winter's very near—

a scary season—
that's the reason
I'm getting out of here."

EIGHT hungry turkeys were on their way to lunch
when one turkey said, "Uh oh, I have a hunch.
Oh no, just look, the pilgrim meal.

Is this Thanksgiving Day?
I remember
one November
I barely got away."

SEVEN hungry turkeys were on their way to lunch
when one turkey said, "Uh oh, I have a hunch.
Invited as a special guest?
Of course, that's what I wish.
But I'm scared stiff.
What if, what if
I'm it—the special dish?"

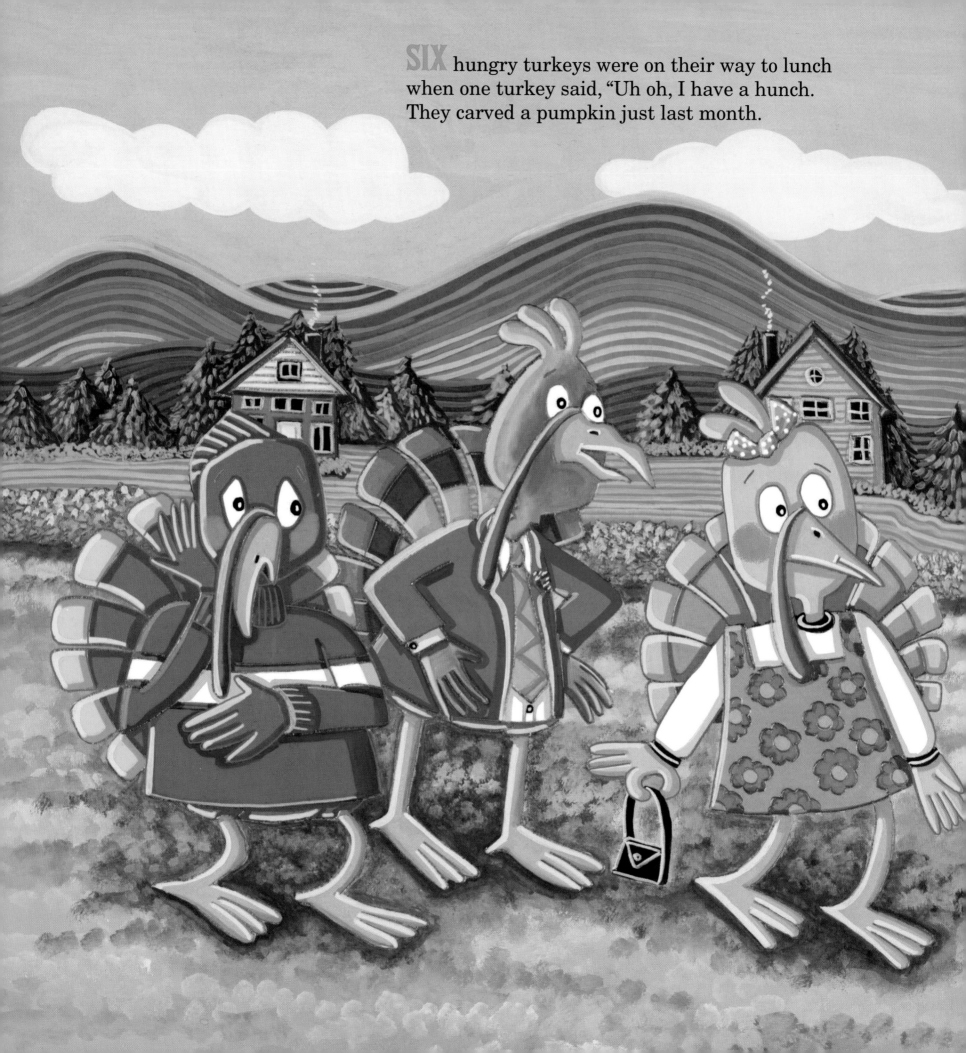

SIX hungry turkeys were on their way to lunch when one turkey said, "Uh oh, I have a hunch. They carved a pumpkin just last month.

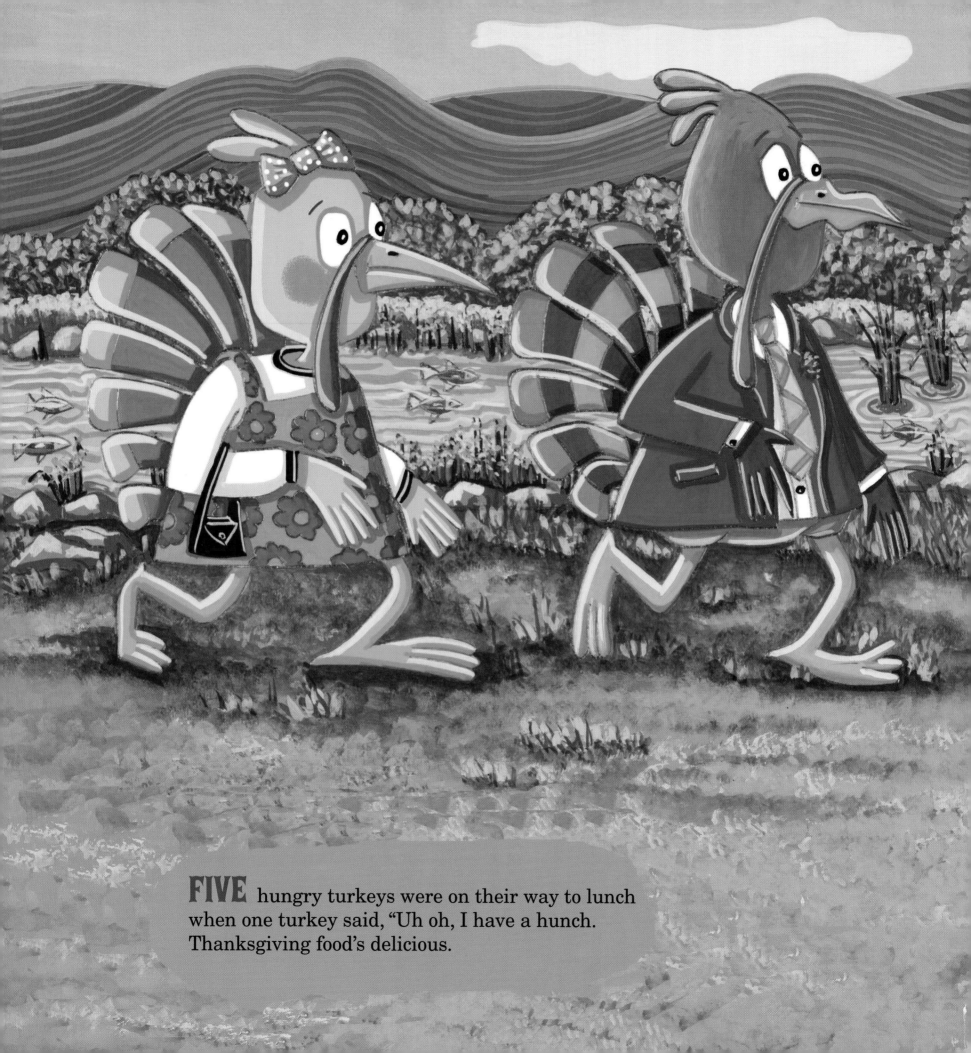

FIVE hungry turkeys were on their way to lunch
when one turkey said, "Uh oh, I have a hunch.
Thanksgiving food's delicious.

Marshmallow yams are yummy.
And if I knew
their whole menu,
I'd go, but I'm no dummy."

FOUR hungry turkeys were on their way to lunch
when one turkey said, "Uh oh, I have a hunch.
Chris P. Byrd's house—straight ahead.

AUTHOR'S NOTE

Ten Hungry Turkeys is the kind of book I love to discover in libraries and stores. My favorites have lots of humor in the words and pictures, something new to learn, and a heavy dose of rhyme and rhythm. All of these qualities appeal to kids too and keep them reading.

In this book, counting backwards is a focus. It's fun and great preparation for the concept of subtraction. More math is slipped in when half (five) of the ten turkeys are gone, and the other five anticipate the promise of twice as much food. A hint of the traditional Thanksgiving story is included, as is a touch of suspense with a happy ending and even a little reward for bravery and gumption!